Roshni
Children's Books

UNESCO WORLD HERITAGE SITES OF INDIA SERIES

United Nations
l, Scientific and
al Organization

SANCHI

Where Tigers Fly and Lions Have Horns

Author **Sohail Hashmi**
Artist **Pervez Rajan**

MAPIN PUBLISHING

Preparations began early for a trip to Sanchi with kids from two primary schools in Bhopal.

A clear blue sky, a mild sun and a pleasant breeze greeted us as we gathered at Gandhi Bhawan. Bhopal was still half asleep when we hopped into our cars and set off on the 48-kilometre drive to Sanchi at seven in the morning.

All the ten children (between 8 and 13 years of age) were excited to be travelling out so early. We were accompanied by Anupama Didi, Priya Didi and Mohsin Bhaiya.

Four of the kids had been to Sanchi when they were 'very young' and had half-forgotten what they had seen, while the others did not know what they were going to see. The joy of going to a new place filled the kids with excitement, which turned into fist-pumping and high-fives when they learnt that there was a mid-way stop for muffins, biscuits and fruit juice.

Everybody was happy but for little Amulya. The poor kid had motion sickness, so we stopped several times. By the time she learnt that she wouldn't feel so bad if she sat in the middle and looked straight ahead, we had already reached Sanchi! Don't feel terribly sorry for her, though; she ate heartily after the walk, and she was fine during the return journey.

The kids were busy finishing their cream-filled biscuits and mango juice when Stupa No. 2 came into view and then slipped out of sight. A little later we entered Sanchi town, and the Great Stupa became visible as we drove past the MP Tourism Resort.

The entire lot was very happy to learn that children have free entry. We drove up the steep kilometre-long path to the gate, although visitors can also walk up.

Once we passed through the metal detector, the stone path took us to the North Gate of the Stupa.

What is a stupa? A stupa is a memorial to Buddha or his great disciples. It is like a halved ball, but unlike a ball, it is not hollow. The outside is covered with bricks or stone slabs.

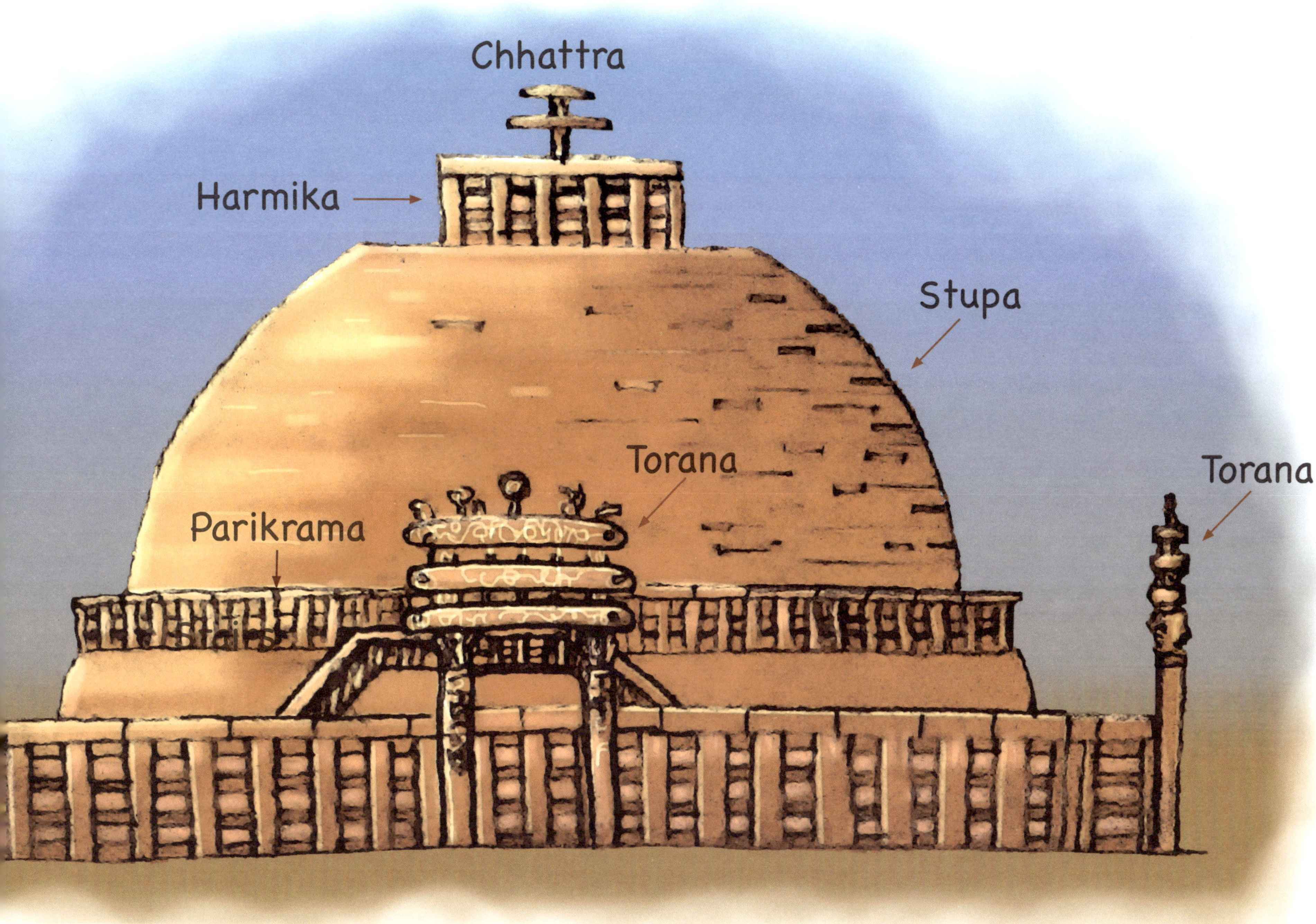
Chhattra
Harmika
Stupa
Torana
Torana
Parikrama
Stairs

The Stupa as seen by an eagle

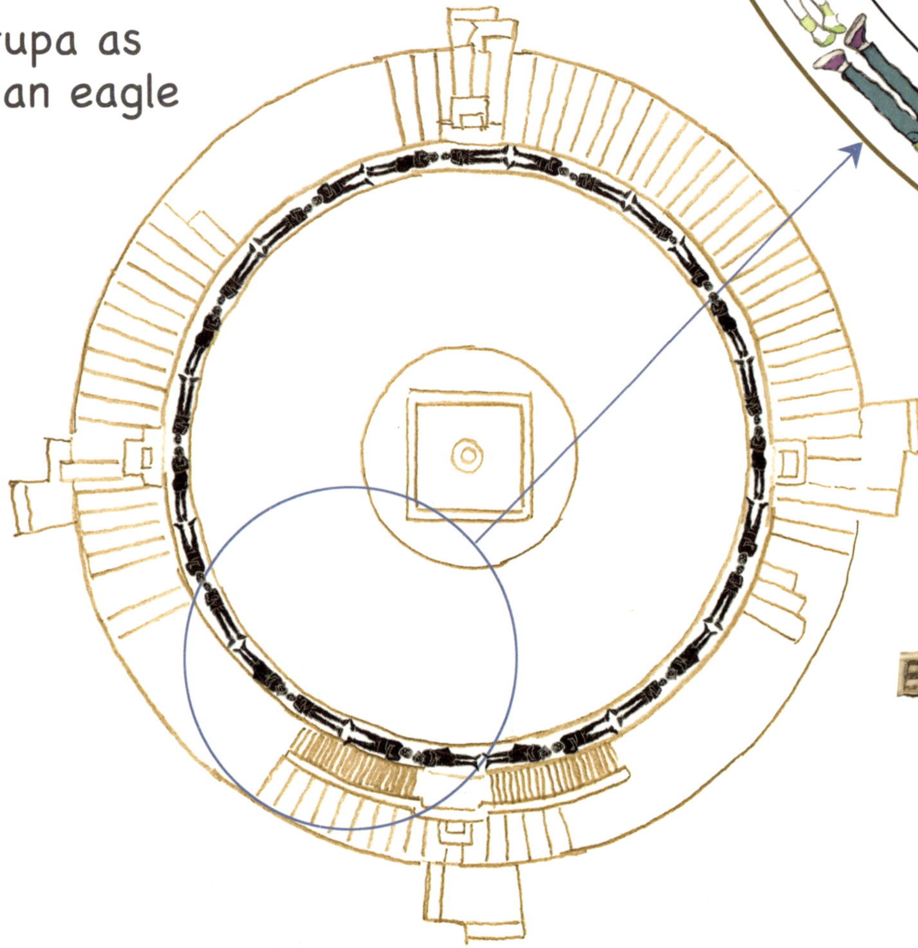

The Great Stupa plays tricks—it seemed to get higher with every step we took! It was twice as high as the gates—16.46 metres. It was so big that to match its circumference twenty-seven 10-year old children would have to lie down in a circle.

The first entry to be built was the South Gate. That the main entry to the Stupa is from the south reminds us that placing the dead body with its feet to the south, and going to burial sites from the south is common to many religions. Do these practices have something to do with the magnetic north?

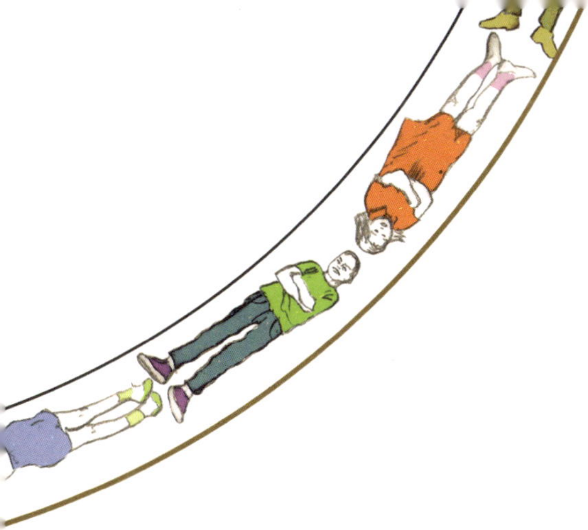

From a distance, the *torana*s or gates looked as high as the Stupa, but in fact, they were around 8.5 metres tall, or almost the combined height of six 10-year-old children.

The gates looked very simple when seen in outline from the road. But when we got closer, we saw that they were crowded with sculptures that seemed almost alive! Sculptures that were above the children's height had to be pointed out by the adults.

The children were not only different ages and heights but they also had different personalities, and this came out in the things that they noticed. They saw things at their eye level and the adults at theirs and so sometimes Sohail would be talking about a carved lion or a buffalo while the children were peering at a lizard crawling below the fence!

In an excited chorus, the children began to list all the things they had seen.

"These women are praying in front of a temple."

"This is a peepal tree."

"That is Hanuman *ji*!"

"There are two Hanuman *ji*s!"

"How do you know that it is Hanuman *ji*?" asked Sohail.

"Looks like him, but his nose is broken," came the reply.

"This is not Hanuman *ji*," explained Sohail. "This is a monkey making an offering to Lord Buddha. And it looks broken because people often touch the sculptures, or perhaps someone hit it with a stone."

Of all the carvings on the North Gate the children were most fascinated by the carvings on the right-hand pillar that shows a monkey offering a bowl of honey to the Buddha. The two monkeys are actually just one monkey; he is first shown going to the Buddha with a bowl in his hand and then he is shown empty-handed.

Did you notice that the Buddha himself is not shown in these carvings? He is shown either as the peepal tree or as the Stupa. It was a long time later—five centuries after his death—that people began to carve images of the Buddha as they imagined he must have looked.

The *Jataka Tales* were stories narrated by the Buddha to explain his teachings. These stories were written down by his disciples and spread far and wide.

Once upon a time, a monkey saw an elephant offering the Buddha water and fruit. The monkey too wanted to make an offering and so presented the Buddha with a honeycomb. The Buddha, however, did not eat the honey. The puzzled monkey then realised that the honeycomb contained insect eggs, which would have been destroyed had the Buddha eaten the honey. So, the monkey removed the eggs and offered the honey again. This time the Buddha gladly accepted the gift. The monkey was so happy that he started dancing and jumping, and then he suddenly slipped and fell to his death. The Buddha was so moved by the monkey's devotion that he predicted the monkey would be reborn in heaven.

The children were still talking about the monkey with the broken nose when Sneha asked, "Sir, why was this gate made?"

"Originally there were no gates and no railings," said Sohail. "When they made the railing, they had to make gates as well. Railings, walls and fences keep you out. Doors, gates and arches allow you in. There are grand gateways in other towns too. I am sure you know their names."

Everybody began to shout together—
"India Gate!" "Gateway of India!" "Buland Darwaza!" "Charminar!"

"Yes," said Sohail, "all of these were built as symbols of love, war, victory or the founding of a city. The gates at Sanchi symbolize the four directions in which the teachings of the Buddha spread."

The pillars of the North Gate have four elephants, just as the pillars of the South Gate have four lions, each facing one of the four directions.

As we turned left at the North Gate, Anikesh, who had been quiet for a while, suddenly stopped and poked his little finger into a circular hole at the base of the Stupa.

"Sir, what are these holes?" he asked.

We had never noticed these holes before! We stopped and looked at them—they were all over the place, just about three feet from the ground.

"These look new," said Sohail, "so maybe they were drilled in the wall to allow rainwater to escape. When it rains, water can enter the Stupa through cracks at the top. If it doesn't flow out, it will keep collecting inside and the Stupa might break because of seepage."

Adults would never have seen these holes because they tend to notice things only at their eye level. Thank you, Anikesh!

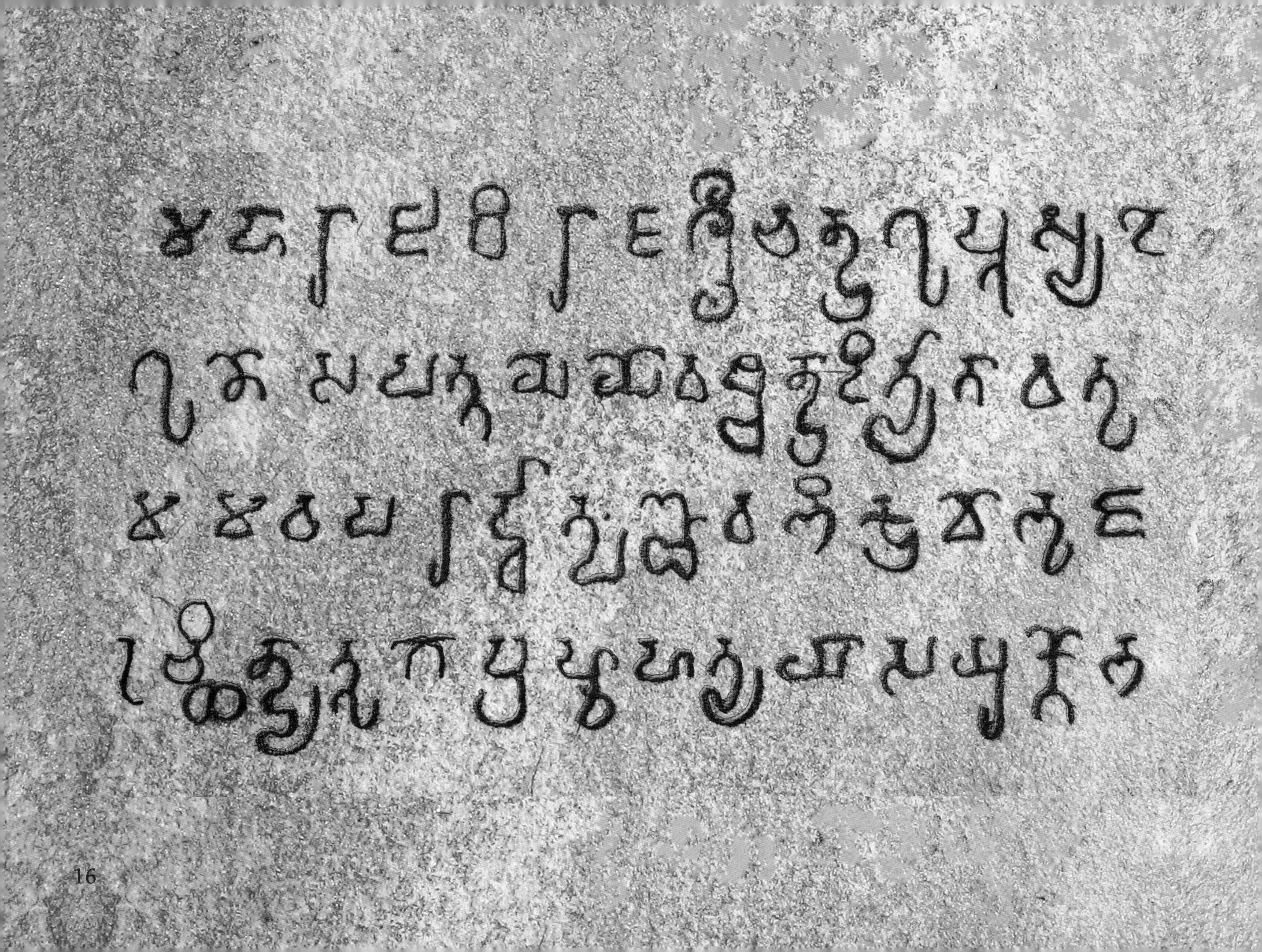

A few steps later, Chandan pointed to a strange script on stones near the base of the Stupa and asked what was written.

"I cannot read it, but I have been told that they are names of people," replied Sohail. "The Stupa was built through public donations and the names of those who gave money were carved in stone on the pillars and on the pavement. Can you guess what script this is?"

"Prakrit?"

"English?"

"Urdu!"

"Prakrit was a language but how was it written?" asked Sohail.

"In Prakrit!" replied the children.

"Well, how do you write Hindi?" asked Sohail.

"In Hindi!"

"No, we write Hindi in Nagri *lipi*, or script," explained Sohail, "and English in Roman script. Urdu is written in Persian script. This is Brahmi *lipi* in which the ancient language Prakrit was written."

As we were discussing Brahmi and Prakrit, Anushka said she was feeling thirsty and so Priya Didi went to fetch her some water.

“All right,” said Sohail, “while we wait for Anushka to drink water, let me show you something here—look at the joints in this stone railing.”

“But that is how they make bamboo cots!” said Rohit.

“Absolutely!” agreed Sohail. “That is how bamboo cots and table and chair joints are made. Such railings were earlier made with wood. Thousands of years passed before people learned to make iron tools and cut stone with chisels to make stone railings. They made railings that were copies of the wooden ones that they had been making for very long. It is actually written on one of the stones at Sanchi that some of the carvers who worked here were originally carvers of ivory and wood.”

While discussing the writings on stone slabs and the construction of railings, we reached the southern pillar of the East Gate. The children noticed a hooded snake with many heads, and the excited chatter started again.

"This is a temple."

"There is a big snake inside!"

"Is that an ice cream cone?"

"There was no ice cream then."

"Those are flames from an *angeethi*."

"Look at all those ducks!"

"No, they are swans. And there are lotuses, too!"

"There is a crocodile."

"No, that is a buffalo, and some people taking a bath in the river."

There were a lot of things there.

What the children were talking about was a story known as the *Miracle of the Serpent*. A poisonous snake had started living in a fire-temple and nobody would go near it. When Gautam Buddha walked into the temple the snake attacked him with smoke and fire, but the Buddha defeated him with the same smoke and fire. The defeated snake then crawled into the begging bowl or *kamandal* of the Buddha.

Sneha suddenly piped up. “Sir, there are so many buffaloes here!”

“You are so right,” said Sohail. “Every time I come here I wonder, there is not a single cow shown anywhere in the Sanchi engravings, but there are buffaloes everywhere! Was Sanchi and the land in this area far wetter 2000 years ago when the Stupa was built?”

Beyond the East Gate, we came to the South Gate, where the stairs to climb up to the *parikrama* start. We climbed up, looking first at the midgets holding up the top beam of the South Gate. These short but very strong imaginary people are called Ganas, and it was believed that the world rested on their shoulders.

An interesting thing to remember is that when Sanchi was being built, many Greeks lived nearby. In fact, Heliodorus the Greek was the ambassador of Takshashila to Vidisha, which was a city near Sanchi. The Greeks believed that one of their gods, Atlas, holds the world on his shoulder. Is it possible that the idea of Ganas holding up the earth on their shoulders came from the Greeks?

Just as there were many Greeks at Sanchi in those times, there were also people from Afghanistan, Iraq, Iran, Mongolia and other places in Asia. The fantastic animals on the gates of the stupas might have been inspired by their sculptures.

We went around the Stupa on the *parikrama* and stopped to look closely at the carvings on the inside of the East Gate, which we had seen earlier from the outside.

We asked the children to make a guess about the theme of these carvings. It was Rohit who made the sharpest observation of the day. He said that all these animals had come for a *darshan* of the Buddha. And he was absolutely right!

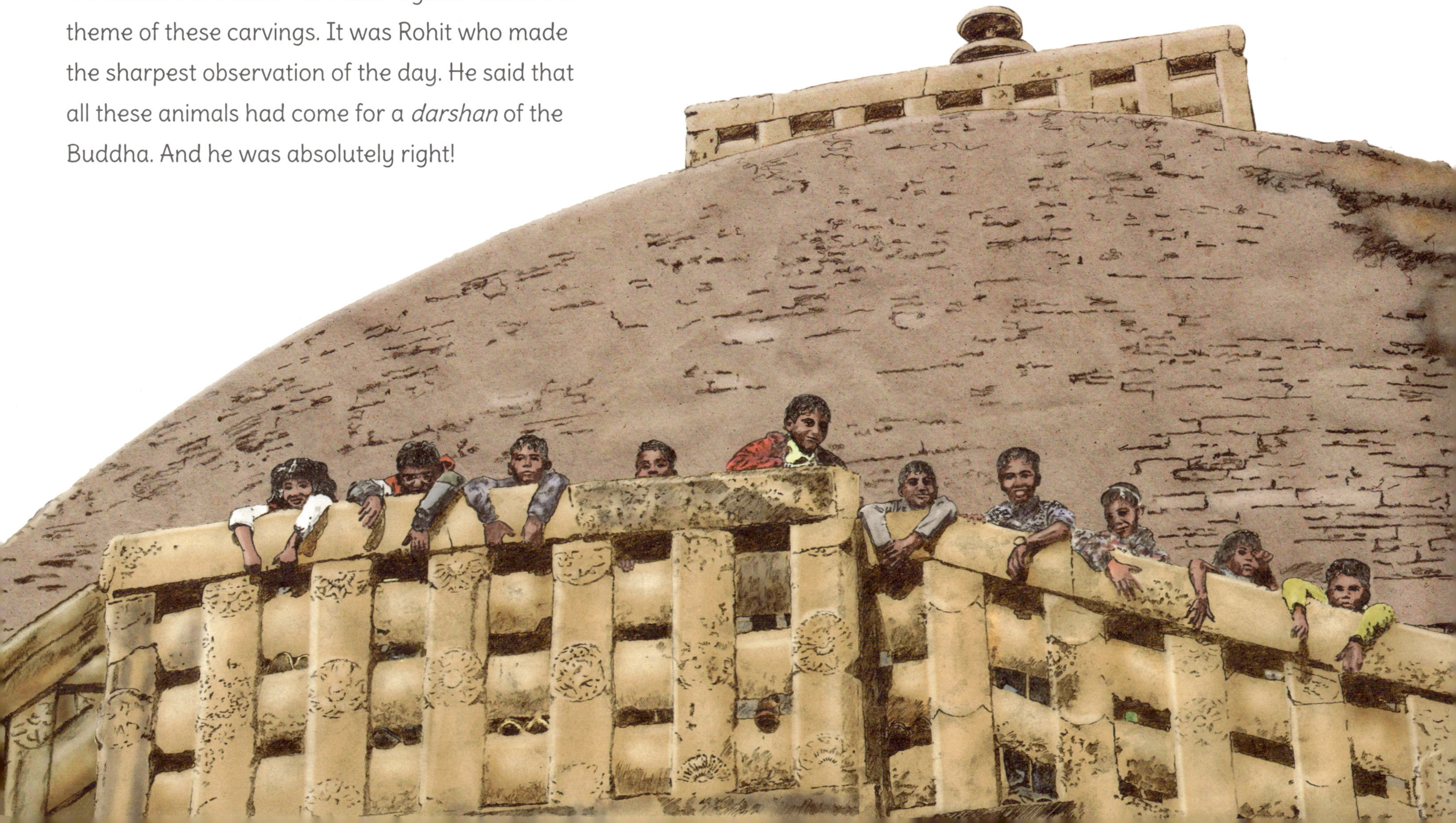

This was the happiest moment of the trip. The children pointed to the large goats with people riding them; two-humped camels; buffaloes; tigers with wings; lions with horns and parrot-like beaks; and sheep with human faces and horns.

There is so much to see at Sanchi—the Great Stupa, several large and small stupas, temples, many sculptures of Buddha (from a later period) and the remains of a monastery.

"What is a monastery?" asked Saransh, who had shown little interest in anything up to now. We had to promise to show him the monastery before we returned.

The monastery at Sanchi does not function anymore, but one can see the ruins of the buildings. Imagine how it would have looked in those days, when it was filled with students and teachers.

People came to monasteries to study about Buddhism and become monks. There were similar schools for girls, called nunneries. The monastery had lecture halls, prayer halls and rooms where the monks slept.

By now, the kids were hungry again, and so we went to the MP Tourism Resort for lunch—a magnificent feast of pizzas, *biryani* and ice cream. These kids could certainly put away quite a bit of food!

After all that talking and feasting, all of them, including little Amulya, slept all the way home. Did Amulya dream she was riding a winged lion?

We need to visit Sanchi again and see all that we missed this time. We will go in the monsoons when Sanchi looks her best. There is plenty more to explore!

Now it is *Your* Turn!

On Top of the Plateau!

How would you escape from an exploding volcano?

Sanchi is located in the Malwa plateau, which is a large area of high, level ground in Madhya Pradesh. This region was full of volcanoes many, many millions of years ago. It is possible that these exploding volanoes also played a part in wiping out the dinosaurs that walked here during that time. Describe the hot, black lava moving like a river!

Can you think of other animals that combine features of different creatures?

Sanchi has carvings of lions with horns and tigers with wings. Many creatures from around the world have fantastical features, such as the sphinx, which has the head of a woman and the body of a lion. Think up more such creatures!

Small vs. Big: which do you prefer?

The carvings at Sanchi are very small in size, even though there are so many of them. Many statues being made nowadays are quite large, and buildings like the Burj Dubai are so tall that they break through the clouds. Do you think large, tall buildings are more thrilling than short ones? Or do short buildings allow us to see more detail? After all, even the tallest man in the world cannot see the top of the Burj!

The word "Sanchi" looks different when it is written in different languages. In how many different ways can you and your friends write "Sanchi"?

How many languages do you know how to write? Write "Sanchi" in as many languages as you can. Maybe you and your friends can even create a new language of your own! Make a simple alphabet for this secret language.

Where have you seen a statue of four lions like the one at Sanchi?

The lion statues at Sanchi once featured four lions set back to back on a decorated base. A similar statue is also the Emblem of India. Sometimes, the animals and designs on a statue or building are associated with certain ideas. For example, the white dove is associated with peace. Can you guess what the different animals and symbols on the Emblem of India mean?

First published in India in 2018 by

Mapin Publishing Pvt. Ltd
706 Kaivanna, Panchvati, Ellisbridge
Ahmedabad 380006 INDIA
T: +91 79 40 228 228
F: +91 79 40 228 201
E: mapin@mapinpub.com
www.mapinpub.com

International Distribution

Worldwide (except North America and South Asia)
Prestel Publishing Ltd.
14-17 Wells Street
London W1T 3PD
T: +44 (0)20 7323 5004
F: +44 (0)20 7323 0271
E: sales@prestel-uk.co.uk

North America
Antique Collectors' Club
T: +1 800 252 5231
F: +1 413 529 0862
E: sales@accpublishinggroup.com
www.accpublishinggroup.com/us

South Asia
Mapin Publishing Pvt. Ltd

ISBN: 978-93-85360-52-7
Series ISBN: 978-93-85360-47-3

Series Editor: Narayani Gupta
Copyediting: Mithila Rangarajan / Mapin Editorial
Design and Production:
Gopal Limbad, Darshit Mori / Mapin Design Studio

Printed in India

The creation of this book was supported by Parag, an initiative of TATA Trusts.

parag
AN INITIATIVE OF TATA TRUSTS

Author: **Sohail Hashmi** loves travelling with family, friends and a camera to explore little-known places across India. He started the "Delhi Heritage Walks with Sohail Hashmi" in 2005 to introduce children, and now adults too, to the wonderful history and heritage of the city. He also makes films to help people learn more about India's culture. He enjoyed writing this book because Sanchi is one of his favourite destinations, with its beautiful, 2000-year old carvings and long history.

Artist: **Pervez Rajan** is an artist who has worked in many cities across India. This is lucky for him, because he also loves to travel and explore new places! He once illustrated the many monuments of Anegundi, near Hampi in Karnataka, to help tourists appreciate the beauty of the place. He is fascinated by details of architecture and carvings, and so depicting the many features of Sanchi was a pleasurable task for him. He hopes to continue to use his art to communicate with a wide range of people.